The NUT That FELL from the TREE

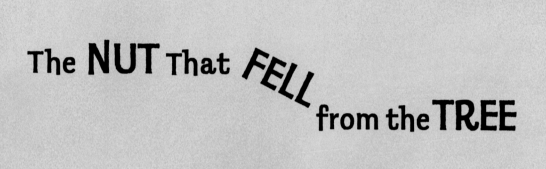

To Hilary — S.B.

To Éva and Zoé. May you grow strong and tall, like an oak tree. — F.C.

Text © 2020 Sangeeta Bhadra
Illustrations © 2020 France Cormier

Kids Can Press gratefully acknowledges the financial
support of the Government of Ontario, through Ontario Creates;
the Ontario Arts Council; the Canada Council for the Arts; and the
Government of Canada for our publishing activity.

Published in Canada and the U.S. by Kids Can Press Ltd.
25 Dockside Drive, Toronto, ON M5A 0B5

Kids Can Press is a Corus Entertainment Inc. company

www.kidscanpress.com

After numerous pencil sketches (many of which were unsatisfactory and
quickly destroyed), the artwork in this book was rendered digitally.
The text is set ITC Klepto.

Edited by Yasemin Uçar
Designed by Marie Bartholomew

Printed and bound in Buji, Shenzhen, China,
in 04/2020 by WKT Company

CM 20 0 9 8 7 6 5 4 3 2 1

LIBRARY AND ARCHIVES CANADA CATALOGUING IN PUBLICATION

Title: The nut that fell from the tree / Sangeeta Bhadra ; illustrations by
France Cormier.
Names: Bhadra, Sangeeta, author. | Cormier, France, 1973— illustrator.
Identifiers: Canadiana 20190213728 | ISBN 9781525301193 (hardcover)
Classification: LCC PS8603.H33 N88 2020 | DDC jC813/.6 — dc23

THE NUT That FELL from THE TREE

Sangeeta Bhadra • France Cormier

Kids Can Press

This is the **house** where Jill plays.

This is the **oak**
that holds the house where Jill plays.

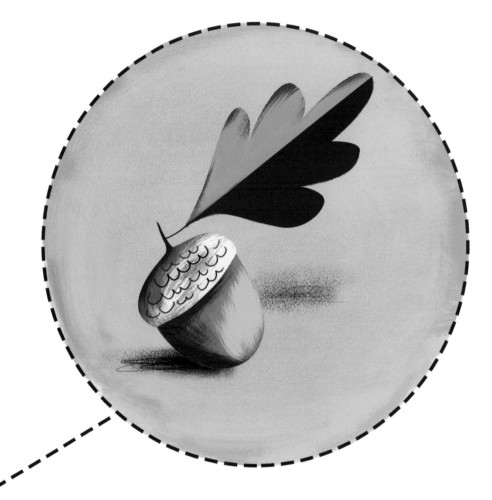

This is the **nut**
that fell from the oak
that holds the house where Jill plays.

This is the **rat** looking out from a shoe
that stole the nut
that fell from the oak
that holds the house where Jill plays.

This is the **jay** with feathers of blue
that swooped in on the rat looking out from a shoe
that stole the nut
that fell from the oak
that holds the house where Jill plays.

This is the **goose** with a bird's-eye view
that ruffled the jay with feathers of blue
that swooped in on the rat looking out from a shoe
that stole the nut
that fell from the oak
that holds the house where Jill plays.

This is the **raccoon**

(a sneak through and through)

that tricked the goose with a bird's-eye view
that ruffled the jay with feathers of blue
that swooped in on the rat looking out from a shoe
that stole the nut
that fell from the oak
that holds the house where Jill plays.

This is the **doe with her fawn** (peek-a-boo!)
that surprised the raccoon (a sneak through and through)
that tricked the goose with a bird's-eye view
that ruffled the jay with feathers of blue
that swooped in on the rat looking out from a shoe
that stole the nut
that fell from the oak
that holds the house where Jill plays.

This is the **bear** — he loves acorns, too! —

ROARRRR!

that chased the doe with her fawn (peek-a-boo!)
that surprised the raccoon (a sneak through and through)
that tricked the goose with a bird's-eye view
that ruffled the jay with feathers of blue
that swooped in on the rat looking out from a shoe
that stole the nut
that fell from the oak
that holds the house where Jill plays.

And this is the **skunk**
that was woken up ...

by this
HULLABALOOOo!

PEE-EW!

Then all was **cold**.

All was **dark**.

All was **still**.

Until ...

This is the **sun**.

This is the **light**
that came from the sun.

This is the **hill**
that shone in the light
that came from the sun.

This is the **nut**
that lay on the hill
that shone in the light
that came from the sun.

This is the **squirrel**
that buried the nut
that lay on the hill
that shone in the light
that came from the sun.

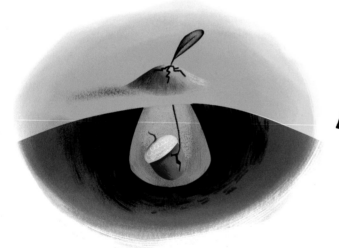

And that little nut grew

and grew

and grew.

This is the **oak**, mighty and tall,
that came from the nut, sturdy and small ...

and now holds the house where Jack plays.